A DINOSAUR NAMED

SUE™

© The Field Museum 1997

THE STORY
OF THE
COLOSSAL FOSSIL

The Field Museum

STONE HOUSE
PRODUCTIONS, LLC

SCHOLASTIC INC. AND THE FIELD MUSEUM PRESENT

A DINOSAUR NAMED

© The Field Museum 1997

THE STORY
OF THE
COLOSSAL FOSSIL

*The World's
Most Complete T. rex*

by Pat Relf
with the SUE Science Team of
The Field Museum
Christopher A. Brochu, Matthew T. Carrano, John J. Flynn,
Olivier C. Rieppel, and William F. Simpson

SCHOLASTIC INC.
New York Toronto London Auckland Sydney Mexico City New Delhi Hong Kong

Library of Congress Cataloging-in-Publication Data available

ISBN 0-439-09985-4

10 9 8 7 6 5 4 3 2 1   00 01 02 03 04 05

Printed in Mexico   49
First printing, September 2000

Table of Contents

Acknowledgments

Amy Louis and Sharon Sullivan of the SUE Project at The Field Museum

Cheryl Carlesimo of Stone House Productions

Susan Hendrickson

The Photography Department of The Field Museum

The Black Hills Institute for permission to use their photos

Bernette Ford, Julie Frazier, Edie Weinberg, and Kimberly Weinberger of Cartwheel Books

The SUE Project was made possible in part by the generous support of the McDonald's® Corporation. 𝕄

The Field Museum

Dear Reader,

Big, fierce animals like lions, tigers, bears (and *Tyrannosaurus rex*) are terrifying. But they are also rare because they are the top predators and scavengers of the "food pyramid." (We feel a lot safer when we walk around because we know how rare they are.) Fossils are pretty uncommon, too, because most animals that die disintegrate before they can become fossilized. This means that when those rare, big, fierce animals die, only a small fraction of them are fossilized. So finding a *T. rex* as huge and complete as SUE is an amazing discovery. Having more than 90% (9 out of 10) of the bones of the largest meat-eating dinosaur is helping our scientific team recover more information about how *Tyrannosaurus* breathed, ate and walked, evolved and lived. And maybe even how one specific, very old animal died!

Because SUE is so well preserved, we've found bones that have never been recovered from a *T. rex* before, and we can pick out new details of the inside and outside of SUE's head and body. Field Museum scientists used old tools, like needles and brushes, and new technologies, like CT scanners, to reveal the stories locked inside SUE's bones. Museums are some of the best places to study extinct animals, because we can compare them to other fossils (or living relatives) in our vast collections and use our laboratories to learn more from them. I am in charge of one of the biggest and best groups of paleontologists in the world, with more than twenty scientists studying SUE and other fossils.

Museums are like giant libraries of specimens—protecting and learning from the only direct record of the history of life through time on our planet. We have more than 150,000 fossils of backboned animals, including SUE, and 21 million other items from nature and human cultures. But when SUE was auctioned, many people worried that the skeleton wouldn't be sold to a museum or college and wouldn't be available for study by scientists (or for you to see on display and in this book). So The Field Museum asked companies like McDonald's and Disney, and other interested people, to help us preserve SUE for you and future generations of kids, adults, and scientists.

Have fun exploring the wonders of SUE—she really is an amazing dinosaur!

John J. Flynn

John J. Flynn
Chairman
Department of Geology
The Field Museum

PROLOGUE

South Dakota, as it was 67 million years ago. The sun shines in a warm, blue sky. Insects buzz and chirp. Birds sing. A low thumping and crunching sound becomes louder and louder, closer and closer. Footsteps! But these are not just any footsteps. These are the footsteps of the largest land predator on Earth. Suddenly the owner of those feet surges into the clearing: the mighty Tyrannosaurus rex, the fearsome king of all dinosaurs. This T. rex is the one that someday will be known as Sue.

Sue moves swiftly on two powerful legs. Hungry, she pauses to sniff the air. There is food nearby! She opens her enormous mouth, showing dozens of huge, pointed teeth. Her jaw can crush the bones of any animal—even another dinosaur. With a grunt, Sue moves off quickly in search of lunch.

If you ask a group of people to name a dinosaur, the answer will probably be *Tyrannosaurus rex.* Everyone knows about *T. rex,* the ferocious lizard king, bad-guy star of books and movies. But what was the real *T. rex* like?

Tyrannosaurus rex were some of the biggest animals ever to walk on two legs. As long as a school bus and just as heavy, *T. rex* truly ruled the earth. Many kinds of dinosaurs had already lived and disappeared in the millions of years before *T. rex* evolved. *T. rex* appeared about 67–70 million years ago and lived in what is now western North America, along with many other kinds of dinosaurs, such as *Triceratops* and *Troodon.* *T. rex* lived on Earth for only about three million years—a short time compared to many other dinosaurs. This was the late Cretaceous Period, just before many of Earth's animals—including *T. rex*—became extinct.

Imagine the astonishment of the people who first found the gigantic bones of a *Tyrannosaurus rex!* That discovery happened just 100 years ago. All that we know about *T. rex* has been learned since that find. Since then, bones from more than twenty different *T. rex* skeletons have been found, including those of the dinosaur we call Sue. But the skeleton of Sue is special. It is the largest, most complete, and best preserved of any *Tyrannosaurus rex* ever found. Imagine all that we can learn from such an amazingly complete skeleton! Studying that skeleton is the job of scientists at The Field Museum in Chicago, where Sue's bones are now on display. At last scientists—and we—have the chance to get to know *T. rex* up close and in more detail than ever before. The story of Sue is a thrilling story of the age of giant dinosaurs, of evolution, and of the amazing achievements of science.

Painter John Gurche worked with the scientists
of The Field Museum to create this portrait
of the Tyrannosaurus rex *named Sue*.

CHAPTER 1
An Amazing Find

When Susan Hendrickson set out for a walk one day with her golden retriever Gypsy, she had no idea that she was about to make a big discovery—the dream of every fossil collector.

Susan had spent the summer of 1990 working with a group of fossil hunters from a company called The Black Hills Institute. All summer, they had camped in tents in the hot, dry hills of western South Dakota. Every day, they searched for fossils such as dinosaur bones. They had found and dug up the bones of some duck-billed dinosaurs called *Edmontosaurus* [ed-MON-toh-SOR-us].

By the end of the summer, the group's work was almost done. The workers were getting ready to pack up and go home. Just before they planned to leave, a tire on the group's truck went flat. Everyone went into town to get the tire fixed—everyone except Susan.

Susan had an idea. The group had searched for fossils nearly everywhere nearby, but there was one area that they had not searched. Across the valley, she could see some cliffs. The group had already found fossils in rock similar to these cliffs. Susan wondered if more fossils might be buried there. This free day, while the others repaired the truck's tire, was her chance to investigate.

There was a thick fog, which is unusual in South Dakota's hot, dry summer. Susan and Gypsy walked together through the fog toward the cliffs. Even walking quickly, it took them more than two hours to hike the seven miles to the cliffs. By that time, the fog was gone and the day was hot and clear.

Susan walked slowly along the base of the cliffs, looking for fossils that might have fallen down the steep hills. The cliffs were striped tan and gray rock. Fossils should be a dark brown.

After fifteen minutes, Susan spotted something. There, on the ground, were some dark brown pieces of bone. Two of the pieces were chunks about two inches (five centimeters) long. There were also some smaller bits of bone. Susan looked up at the cliff to see where these bones had come from. There, about eight feet (less than three meters) above her head, were more brown bones sticking out of the cliff wall. She hoped that there would be more bones from this animal buried inside the cliff.

Excited, Susan climbed up. She looked closely. The bones sticking out of the cliff were huge. She could see three backbones, a leg bone, and a rib. The bones were hollow, which showed that they came from a meat-eating dinosaur. Susan knew that the only big, meat-eating dinosaur that had lived in this part of North America was *Tyrannosaurus rex*. This could be a fantastic discovery. And it was!

opposite & above: Susan Hendrickson at the cliff where Sue was found.
below: Some of Sue's visible bones.

Tyrannosaurus rex was first discovered in Wyoming in 1900. From that time until Susan's discovery in 1990, there had been only twenty-two partial (at least 20% complete) skeletons of *T. rex* ever found, so finding any *T. rex* fossils was a very important discovery. Although the crew did not know whether the dinosaur that Susan had found was male or female, they named it "Sue" in her honor.

Some of the work crew had to leave at the end of the summer. So Susan and just a few other workers started digging for the *Tyrannosaurus rex* bones.

As they looked at the bones that stuck out from the cliff, they could see that the fossils were buried under twenty-five to thirty feet (eight to nine meters) of rock and dirt. All of that rock needed to be removed before they could reach the rest of the bones. Big, heavy machines might damage the bones, so the crew

moved all of the rocky earth with handheld tools. They broke up the rock with picks. They pried away huge pieces of rock with crowbars and pushed them down the hill. They dug with shovels. They worked from first light until sunset in the blazing hot sun.

In just a few days of hard work, the diggers reached the level of the bones. Now they worked more gently. With picks, smaller shovels, small hammers, chisels, and even brushes, they removed most of the rock around the bones.

The workers were amazed as they uncovered more and more bones. Earlier *Tyrannosaurus rex* finds had been just a few bones, or skeletons with more than half the bones missing. But this time the diggers found nearly all of the animal's bones. It was the most complete *T. rex* skeleton ever! Paleontologists [PAY-lee-on-TALL-o-jists], the scientists who study fossils to learn about the history of life on Earth, would be thrilled to have such a complete skeleton to study.

The size of the bones also surprised everyone. The skull was enormous, nearly five feet (1.5 meters) long. The leg bones were huge. One toe claw was seven inches (eighteen centimeters) long. In fact, Sue was the largest *T. rex* ever found.

The bones were in excellent condition, too. Fossil collectors are used to finding broken, chipped, or even crushed bones. But most of these bones were in amazingly good shape. The huge skull even had most of its teeth, although many had been smashed or had fallen out of the sockets in the skull.

opposite & right: Susan and the crew at work removing Sue from her fossil bed.
below: Sue's enormous skull uncovered in its rocky resting place.

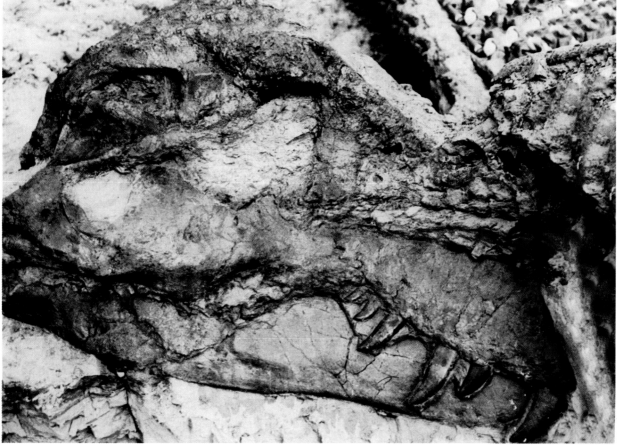

As the workers dug, they photographed the area to record where the bones were lying. They numbered the bones and wrote their locations in a notebook. This information would be very important to scientists later, as they studied the fossils and how they fit together. Many of the bones lay exactly as they had the day Sue died. Bones from the tail lay in a curved line. Some neck vertebrae lay together. But other bones were jumbled. Some of the dinosaur's hip bones were found on top of its skull, for example. A few pieces were missing: one of Sue's arms, a few backbones and ribs. Only one bone of the left foot was found.

Among the *Tyrannosaurus rex* bones, the diggers also found fossils of plants and other animals that had lived at the same time as Sue, about 67 million years ago. Near Sue's bones, they discovered the bones of duck-billed, plant-eating dinosaurs, as well as fossilized leaves,

pieces of wood, pinecones, and the skull of a turtle. They carefully saved these fossils for later study by scientists.

When the diggers removed a bone, they tried to keep some of the rock around it, too. The rock would support the bone, and the fossil would be less likely to break. Later, at a laboratory, workers could spend as much time as they needed to remove the remaining rock very carefully.

If a bone looked especially fragile, the workers coated it with thin but very strong glue to keep it from splintering or flaking. Next, they put a layer of aluminum foil on the bone. Finally, they covered the whole thing with burlap soaked in plaster. Plaster is a white goop that dries extremely hard and is often used by doctors to make casts for people's broken arms and legs. The hard burlap and plaster coating, or "jacket," would protect Sue's bones on the trip

back to the laboratory. The diggers labeled each plaster jacket with the same number as the bone inside the plaster.

The bones, in their plaster jackets, were loaded onto trucks. The biggest piece of rock, the one containing Sue's skull and hip bones, weighed four tons. The trucks delivered the bones to the offices of The Black Hills Institute about 150 miles (240 kilometers) away. There, specialists in fossil cleaning called preparators [pre-PAR-uh-tors] began the long and difficult process of cleaning the last bits of rock away from the bones. Suddenly, trouble began.

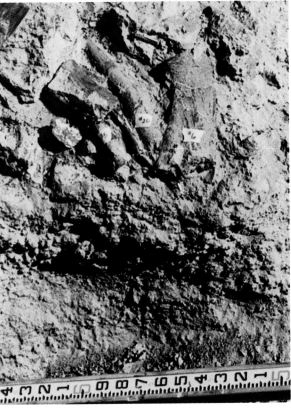

above: The crew at work excavating Sue
from her fossil bed.
right: These rib fragments were among
the first bones to be excavated.
opposite: The crew exposes the skull and vertebrae
of Sue's enormous, curved tail.

The Black Hills Institute preparators had made a good start at cleaning the bones when the F.B.I. and other government officials arrived with legal papers that allowed them to seize the fossils. They took all of the bones and stored them in Rapid City, South Dakota, thirty miles (fifty kilometers) away. Although the Institute had paid some money to the owner of the land, it was not clear exactly who owned the bones, or whether the Institute had legally bought them. In addition, the landowner was part Native American, a member of the Sioux tribe. The Sioux tribe said that the bones really belonged to the tribe. Everyone wanted to own this amazing dinosaur!

The arguments wound up in the law courts. For five years, lawyers for all the would-be owners argued in court. Meanwhile, Sue's bones sat safely in storage at the South Dakota School of Mines and Technology in Rapid City. No one could clean them or study them until ownership was established.

At last the judge decided: Sue's bones belonged to the owner of the land, not to The Black Hills Institute or the Sioux tribe. He was free to keep them or sell them. Finally he decided to sell them. The United States government decided the landowner would get the fairest price at an auction. In October 1997, seven years after Susan Hendrickson first spotted the bones, the skeleton went up for auction in New York City.

The auction house, Sotheby's, put the *Tyrannosaurus rex* skull on display for everyone to see. Many people came to look. Many people wanted to buy the skeleton. Several museums wanted to make Sue the star of their exhibits. Wealthy dinosaur lovers wanted to add Sue to their own private collections. Everyone knew that Sue was worth a lot of money, but no one knew how much, as a specimen like this had never been sold before. At an auction, Sue would go to the person or group that was willing—and able—to pay the highest price. Scientists everywhere were extremely worried

A DINOSAUR NAMED SUE:

that Sue would end up in a private collection. If she did, scientists might not be able to study the bones and learn all that this fantastic discovery could tell them about *T. rex*. And ordinary people might never see the amazing sight of the world's most complete *T. rex* skeleton.

In Chicago, the scientists of The Field Museum also worried about this. They wanted the bones to go to a place where scientists could always study them and dinosaur lovers could always see them. But they knew that most museums, including theirs, could not afford to pay the price that a very rich private collector could. They had an idea. They asked companies and other supporters to give the museum money to help them to buy Sue. With help, perhaps The Field Museum could make the highest bid on Sue.

At last the day of the auction arrived. The auction house was crowded with people who

hoped to bid on Sue. Other bidders called in by telephone. Newspaper and television reporters came to watch the auction and all the excitement. The auctioneer started the bidding at half a million dollars. The bids went up quickly, $100,000 or more at a time. The bids went higher and higher, into the millions of dollars. One by one, the bidders dropped out as the price became too high for them. At last only one bidder was left. After just nine minutes of bidding, The Field Museum had offered the highest price: more than eight million dollars! With the help of the McDonald's Corporation, Walt Disney World Resorts, and other donors, The Field Museum had bought Sue.

---

above: The exciting auction took place more than seven years after Sue was discovered.
opposite: Sue's massive skull on display after the auction.

Dinosaur lovers everywhere celebrated because now anyone would be able to see Sue's skeleton at The Field Museum in Chicago, or an exact copy at Walt Disney World, or in one of the traveling shows that McDonald's would sponsor. Scientists were happy because, at the museum, Sue's bones would always be available for study. The scientists of The Field Museum were happiest of all, because they would have the opportunity of a lifetime: to prepare and study the world's most complete *Tyrannosaurus rex* skeleton, and to share it with the world.

In addition to the auction price, The Field Museum had to raise the money that would be needed for the museum to clean and study the bones and to put them together into a permanent exhibit at the museum. That meant hiring extra preparators and other scientists, building special laboratories, and buying new equipment. The funds would also allow the museum to prepare other fossils for display and research. Scientists at the museum were eager to get started.

How do you move the world's most valuable dinosaur? The museum hired a special moving company that is capable of moving delicate paintings and sculptures. The bones themselves were covered in their protective plaster jackets. Field Museum preparators went to the auction company storehouse to make the original plaster jackets stronger. Then the movers and museum scientists carefully strapped each bone into a wooden crate lined with plastic foam. The crates containing Sue's bones filled an entire moving truck. A moving truck is special because it has air cushions on its rear axle. Like little pillows, the air cushions squish when the truck hits a bump, so that the boxes inside have a smooth and gentle ride.

At long last, the truck carrying Sue arrived in Chicago. Trying hard to contain their excitement, The Field Museum scientists moved the crates into a specially prepared area of the museum. They even had to knock a huge hole in a wall to make a door big enough for Sue to fit through! Now the huge task of cleaning and preparing the bones—and the wonderful chance to study them—would begin.

above & opposite:
Sue arrives at The Field Museum.

TRIASSIC

JURASSIC

248 MYA   206 MYA   144 MYA

CHAPTER 2
When Sue Roamed the Earth

N o wonder scientists were excited to see Sue's bones. Studying these well-preserved bones is like looking back through millions of years to the time when dinosaurs lived in what is now North America.

The name dinosaur means "fearfully great reptile." What are dinosaurs? Dinosaurs are part of the reptile group of animals. Modern reptiles include crocodiles, turtles, snakes, lizards, and birds. Dinosaurs have certain bone structures that are different from other reptiles. Dinosaurs have holes in their hip sockets, for example — something you can see in the bones of chickens or turkeys, which are living dinosaurs.

The first dinosaurs lived about 230 million years ago. Some of the very earliest known dinosaurs have been found in Madagascar, a big island near Africa, by scientists from The Field Museum. At the time of the first dinosaurs, most of the earth was very hot and dry. Other reptiles

were much more common than dinosaurs. But as the earth slowly changed, its climate in many places became less harsh — less dry and hot — and just right for dinosaurs.

The greatest time for dinosaurs was from the late Jurassic [juh-RASS-ic] Period, 145 million years ago, until the end of the Cretaceous [kre-TAY-shus] Period, 65 million years ago. Many different kinds of dinosaurs evolved during this time. *Brachiosaurus* [BRAK-ee-o-SOR-us], first discovered by a scientist from The Field Museum, had a very long neck that let it eat tall plants. *Allosaurus* [AL-uh-SOR-us] was a meat-eater. Both of these dinosaurs lived in what is now North America. But they had disappeared long before *Tyrannosaurus rex* lived on Earth.

The Earth, its climate, and its plants changed, and so did the animals that lived on Earth. Flowering plants first evolved in the Cretaceous Period, and the later plant-eating dinosaurs,

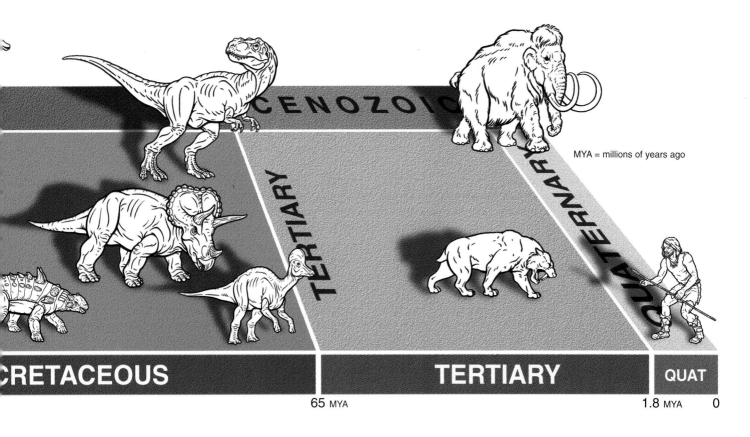

CENOZOIC

TERTIARY

QUATERNARY

MYA = millions of years ago

| CRETACEOUS | TERTIARY | QUAT |

65 MYA   1.8 MYA   0

such as the duck-billed hadrosaurs [HAD-ruh-sors], thrived on a diet of flowers and conifers. It was at this time, during the later part of the Cretaceous Period, that a very big meat-eater also emerged in North America—*Tyrannosaurus rex.*

What was Sue's world like? Today, the Great Plains stretch over the middle of North America. This area is dry and hot in the summer, but cold and snowy in the winter. It looked very different when Sue was alive, about 67 million years ago. What is now the Great Plains was mostly covered by a great, shallow sea. To the west, the Rocky Mountains were still pushing their way upward. Volcanoes erupted where Idaho and Nevada are today. There were no snowy winters. The weather was damp and quite warm all year round—more like Georgia or South Carolina are today. Rivers ran down from the nearby hills. They carved canyons and valleys into the hills, and washed mud and sand down to the sea.

This warm, damp climate was like a green-house for plants. Fossils of plants from this time tell scientists that there were forests of trees—magnolia, oak, sycamore, hickory, birch, and conifers or evergreens. In the swamps, trees similar to modern sequoia [suh-KWOY-uh] and cypress trees grew tall. There were ferns, vines, and many small, shrubby flowering plants. Poison ivy grew in the forests, and water lilies floated in swamps and lakes. But, even though today many kinds of grasses cover this area, there was not a single blade of grass anywhere at this time! Grasses did not evolve until much later.

Sue's world was full of other animals, too. Flying insects such as bees, dragonflies, and butterflies flitted from flower to flower. Beetles, roaches, and even termites crawled about. The ancestors of today's opossums and smaller mammals lived in the forests. There were no large mammals like today's bears or elephants. But many birds flew in the air or waded in the water. Snakes, crocodiles, turtles, frogs, and salamanders were all around.

Flying reptiles called pterosaurs [TEH-ruh-sors] glided through the air. They had long crests on their heads. Pterosaurs varied in size. Some were small, like chickens, while others were huge. From wing tip to wing tip, a large pterosaur was about thirty-five feet (eleven meters) across—almost the size of a small airplane! Some kinds had no teeth, but probably ate many different animals, including fish and insects.

The sea was full of life. There were sharks, jellyfish, crabs, and rays. True lizards called mosasaurs also lived in the ocean. They were marine lizards closely related to the family of lizards which include the Komodo dragon. Other aquatic reptiles, the long-necked plesiosaurs [PLEE-zee-o-sors], used their flippers to "fly" through the water.

Many land reptiles were neighbors of *Tyrannosaurus rex*. *Triceratops* were huge, plant-eating dinosaurs. They grew to thirty feet (ten meters) long. *Triceratops* had three horns and a big frill shielding the back of their heads.

There were several kinds of hadrosaurs. All of these plant-eating dinosaurs had duck-like bills, and some had fancy crests on their heads, such as the horn-crested *Parasaurolophus* [PAR-uh-sor-OL-uh-fuss].

Ankylosaurs [an-KI-lo-sores] are sometimes called armored dinosaurs because they were covered with hard, bony plates. Spikes lined the backs of some ankylosaurs, and horns at the back of their heads also helped to protect them. Only their bellies were unprotected. In order to wound this big, heavy dinosaur, another animal would have had to flip it over! Although they looked frightening, ankylosaurs were strictly plant-eaters.

Like its neighbor *Tyrannosaurus rex*, *Troodon* [TROE-o-don] was a meat-eater. But *Troodon* was much smaller than *T. rex*—about the size of a human being. (Of course, no human beings lived at the time of these dinosaurs.) *Troodon* moved fast, and it had long, sharp claws.

The most awesome of all dinosaur species, though, was *Tyrannosaurus rex*. Individuals of this species could grow to more than forty feet (twelve meters) long—as long as a school bus,

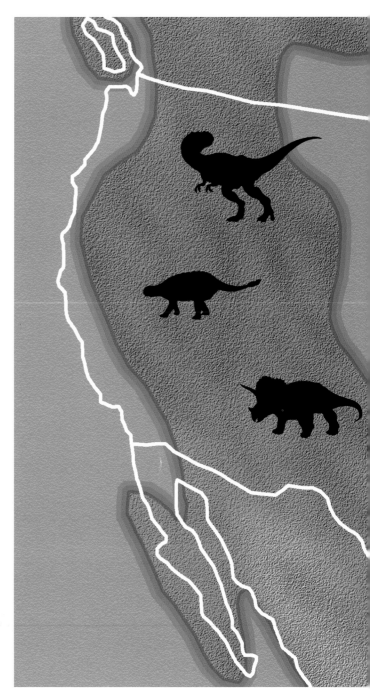

and just as heavy! The 20th-century scientists who first found its enormous bones gave it the name *Tyrannosaurus rex*, scientific Latin words that mean "tyrant lizard king." A tyrant is a ruler who is powerful and cruel—like the appearance of this immense meat-eating dinosaur. *Tyrannosaurus rex* is often called *T. rex* for short.

Tyrannosaurus rex was the biggest species of meat-eating, land animal of its time. It stood on its huge back legs, holding its tail up. Though *T. rex* was enormous, it may have been quite

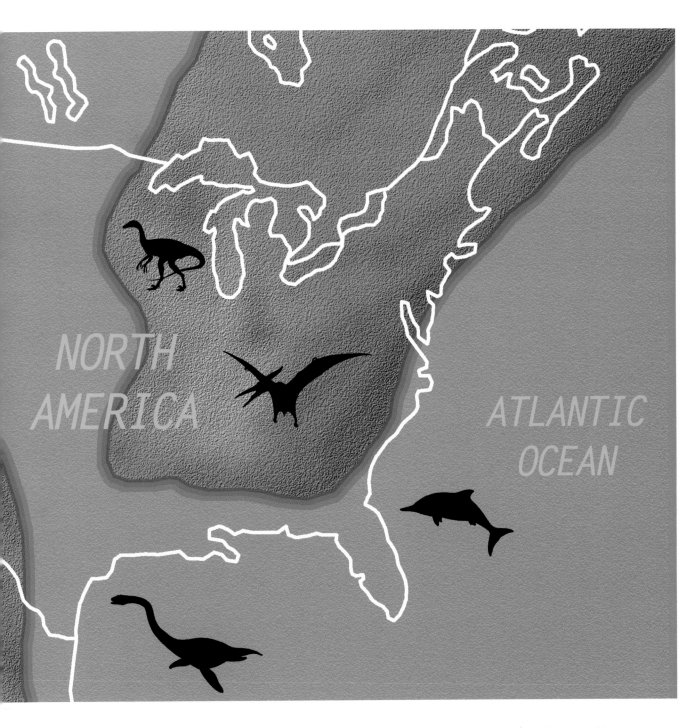

NORTH
AMERICA

ATLANTIC
OCEAN

speedy. It ate other animals, including dinosaurs such as *Triceratops*. *T. rex*'s powerful jaws and gigantic teeth easily tore other animals to shreds. Those mighty jaws could even crunch through bones when necessary.

Tyrannosaurus rex may have lived in family groups, although we do not have proof of this yet. The females almost certainly laid eggs, from which babies hatched. A *T. rex* might live for many years, and it continued to grow almost its entire life. This species of enormous dinosaur

lived on Earth for about three million years—thirty times as long as the modern human species has lived on Earth so far! During that time, they certainly were the kings of dinosaurs.

The white outline shows North America today. Underneath, we see this area as it was when Sue was alive, with blue seas covering the middle part of the continent.

*A 1920s classical interpretation of Tyrannosaurus rex
and Triceratops by painter Charles Knight,
from the collection of The Field Museum.*

A DINOSAUR NAMED SUE:

How do scientists know what Tyrannosaurus rex *was like?* Paleontologists first found fossilized *T. rex* bones in 1900. Since then, they have found and studied twenty-two different sets of bones from partial *T. rex* skeletons, including Sue. Sue is the most complete *T. rex* ever discovered. Little by little, paleontologists have learned more and more about what *T. rex* was like. Here are some of the questions they have tried to answer.

How did Tyrannosaurus rex *stand?* Years ago, drawings showed *T. rex* standing up very tall, with their heads up high and their tails dragging on the ground, like the *T. rex* in the background. Scientists now know that *T. rex* held their long, strong tails off the ground, like the *T. rex* in the foreground, because fossilized tracks of big, meat-eating dinosaurs show only footprints—no trails of tails dragging behind. Scientists believe that *T. rex* stood in the same posture as today's birds, with their backbones forming a tilted S shape.

What did Tyrannosaurus rex eat? The huge serrated, or jagged, teeth of *T. rex* show that they were meat-eaters. Plant-eaters usually have flat teeth for grinding leaves and stalks. *T. rex* may have been hunters, for they probably could move quickly enough to kill a live animal. Or they may have been scavengers, eating animals that were already dead. Studies of Sue's skull have shown that *T. rex* had an incredible sense of smell. That would have been useful for either hunting or scavenging. Their eyes faced forward, giving good depth perception — the ability to tell how far away something is. That is useful for hunters, but it could be useful for scavengers, too. It is likely that *T. rex* both hunted and scavenged. Nearly all large, meat-eating animals today — such as hyenas and lions — do both to ensure that they have plenty of food.

If *Tyrannosaurus rex* were hunters, they were very fierce ones. Their teeth were huge. Sue's largest tooth was as long as your hand — six inches (fifteen centimeters) long — and that was just the part that showed! The other half of that tooth was inside the jaw, making the whole tooth more than one foot (thirty centimeters) long! Like many animals (but not mammals, including humans!), reptiles lose teeth throughout their lives.

New teeth constantly grow in to replace them. Sue's skull shows that new teeth were growing in, even at the time she died.

Scientists know at least two of the animals that *T. rex* ate, because bones of those animals have been found with huge teeth marks in them! *Tyrannosaurus rex* fed on *Triceratops* and a type of hadrosaur called *Edmontosaurus* [ed-MON-toh-SOR-us]. In addition, many tiny pieces of the bones of another plant-eating dinosaur were found in the fossilized droppings of what is thought to be a *T. rex*. That means that the fearsome teeth of *T. rex* not only tore through muscle, but crunched through bone as well.

Studies show that *T. rex* may have had the strongest bite of any animal ever — including living alligators, lions, and sharks.

above: One of Sue's enormous teeth (actual size).
right: Despite Sue's enormous size, this illustration shows the surprising comparison between the size of a human arm (right) and Sue's arm (left).

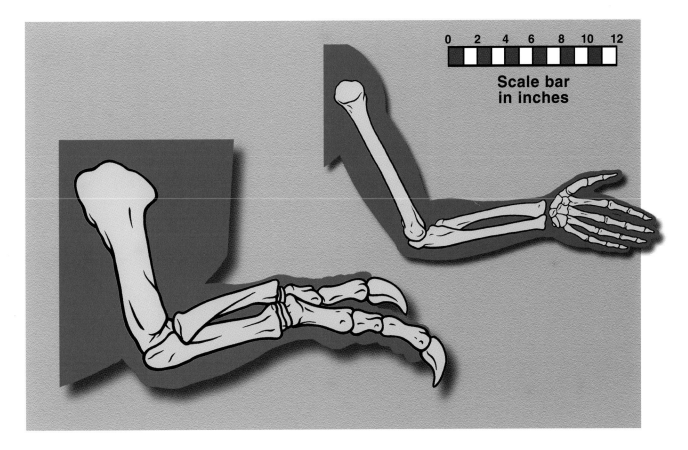

0 2 4 6 8 10 12

**Scale bar
in inches**

What did Tyrannosaurus rex's small arms do? No one knows yet. Sue's arms are only the second ones ever discovered for a *T. rex*. Compared to *T. rex*'s huge legs, its arms were very small. Yet the spots on the bones where muscles attached show that the arms had very strong, powerful muscles. The arms clearly were used for something, and as scientists study Sue's bones further, they may learn more.

Was Tyrannosaurus rex *warm-blooded or cold-blooded*? For many years, scientists figured that dinosaurs were cold-blooded, like modern reptiles — that is, their bodies warmed or cooled depending on the temperature around them. Modern reptiles such as snakes and lizards like to bask in the sun for this reason. Birds and mammals, including humans, are warm-blooded — that is, their bodies heat and cool themselves in order to stay at about the same temperature all the time. But now scientists are not so sure that some dinosaurs such as *T. rex* were cold-blooded. Cold-blooded animals tend to be slow-moving, but many dinosaurs seem to have

been able to move very quickly. Also, dinosaur bones have been found in places that were quite cold when the dinosaurs were alive. Those places would not have been good homes for cold-blooded animals. In addition, scientists have realized that the closest relatives of *T. rex* today are birds, not crocodiles, lizards, and snakes — and birds are warm-blooded. In addition, fossils of some small, active dinosaurs have recently been discovered with feathers, just as birds use feathers for insulation. So we do not know for sure whether *T. rex* was warm- or cold-blooded.

Did Tyrannosaurus rex *lay eggs*? Scientists are not absolutely certain whether *T. rex* laid eggs or gave birth to live babies. Since modern relatives such as birds and crocodiles lay eggs, and since eggs have been found for many species of both meat-eating and plant-eating dinosaurs, it seems almost certain that *T. rex* would have laid eggs, too. But, so far, no fossilized *T. rex* eggs have been found.

Was Sue male or female? No one knows yet. The skeleton was named Sue, after the woman who discovered it. Some scientists think that Sue's large size and sturdy bones show that "she" really was female. For some modern animals, such as owls, the female usually is larger than the male. But for other animals, such as crocodiles, the male is generally larger in size. So, for now, scientists are uncertain about Sue's gender. It is possible that we will never be certain of Sue's, and most dinosaur species', gender.

When did Sue live? Scientists know that she lived close to 67 million years ago because of the age of the rock around her bones. Geologists are scientists who study the earth. They can tell how old rock is by comparing the different layers of rock with the layers in other places, or by using special kinds of dating techniques. Other fossils also help scientists to know when a particular layer of rock was formed, because different species of plants and animals lived at different times. Of course, no one knows the exact dates of Sue's life. When scientists say millions of years ago, they are really talking about an estimate varying by tens of thousands to a few hundred thousand years.

How old was Sue when she died? Sue herself certainly was very old when she died. Of the twenty-two *Tyrannosaurus rex* skeleton finds so far, Sue is the biggest specimen. That tells us that she was also the oldest. Also, some of Sue's bones had started to grow together. Her spine, hip, and shoulder bones showed signs of this. This happens later in life in many reptiles, so that, too, tells us that Sue was old. We do not know exactly how long she lived—probably tens of years—but it was a long time for a *T. rex*.

Did Sue have any injuries? During her long life, Sue had her share of problems. Field Museum scientists have not seen any scars on Sue's bones that they believe definitely came

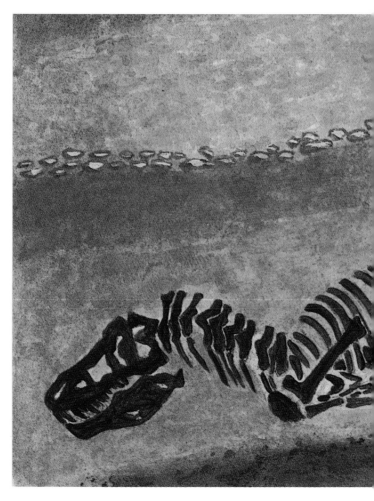

from fights with other animals. But there are scars on her bones showing that Sue had had some diseases—perhaps infections or even "cancers." Her jaw, her leg, her arm, and perhaps her tail show signs of this. Some of her bones were injured, showing signs of breakage and healing. Some of her teeth, too, show signs of disease. One tooth is only two inches long (that was short for Sue's teeth!) and twisted. No one yet knows what caused this.

How did Sue die? The bones show no sign of a big fight with another animal. She might have died of disease. But Sue was so old that she simply may have died of old age. The fossilized plants found among her bones and the surrounding sediments and rocks tell us that she died next to a river.

Because almost all of Sue's bones were in one spot, scientists know that Sue's body was covered by sand and mud very soon after she died.

The fact that this happened so quickly was lucky for us, because Sue's body was buried before other animals could carry away her bones. Sue was dead before the sand and mud covered her, because the moving sand and water tumbled her bones slightly. Sue's hip bones were found near and on top of her skull, and her leg bones were mixed with her ribs, for example.

What happened then? Sue's skin and muscles and organs rotted away. Just her bones were left, covered with sand and mud. Over thousands of years, more layers of mud and sand collected on top of Sue's bones. The weight of these layers pressed down on the sand. The sand became a rock called sandstone. The bones became darker, heavier, more brittle, and very much like rock. That is, they became fossils.

We are lucky to have fossils at all, because conditions must be just right for them to be preserved. If a dead animal is not covered quickly, other animals may take the bones away. If the bones lie in the open air, they dry up and break apart. If they remain in ordinary soil, they may rot. Only if they are covered quickly can they turn to fossils. No wonder it is so unusual to find a nearly complete fossilized skeleton! Sue is a real prize.

For millions of years, Sue's fossilized bones lay buried in the sandstone. Earthquakes and volcanoes squeezed the earth of the western United States in great folds and cracks. Some layers of earth were pushed downward, deeper into the Earth's crust, while other layers were pushed upward. The great sea that once covered so much of North America dried out. The swamps and rivers dried up. The climate became colder. Wind and rain battered the land, wearing away the soft sandstone. Slowly, the side of the hill containing Sue's bones eroded away. A few of the bones fell down the cliff and landed . . . well, they landed just where Susan Hendrickson and Gypsy went for a walk one day.

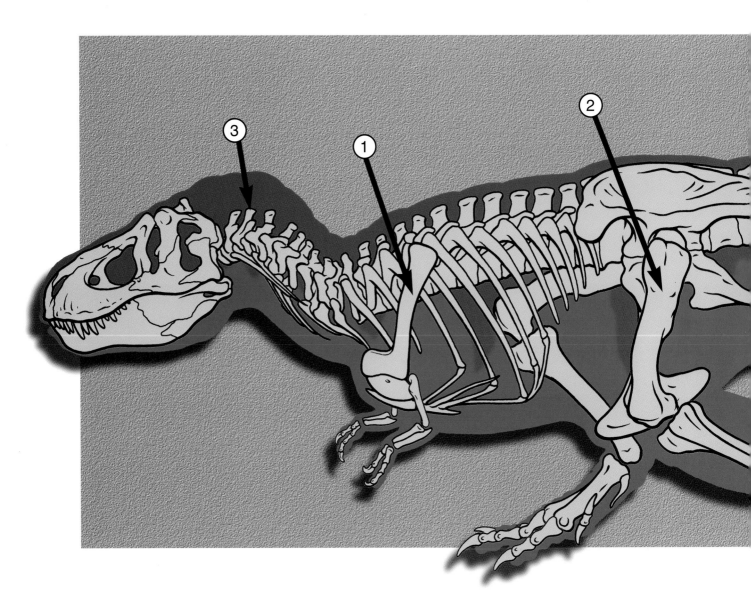

Tyrannosaurus rex lived on Earth for about three million years, during the late Cretaceous Period. The golden age of dinosaurs was ending. There were not as many different kinds of dinosaurs as there once had been. Some had become extinct. But at the very end of the Cretaceous Period, something strange happened. Nearly all of the remaining non-flying dinosaurs died around the same time. Many other animals such as pterosaurs, plesiosaurs, most small ocean-dwelling species, and some families of fish, birds, and mammals died out at that time, too. In addition to the smaller animals that died out, most species of large animals of that time became extinct. Even some kinds of plants died out. The layer of rock from that time contains unusual chemicals. Something—or a number of things —happened.

Some scientists believe that an asteroid hit the Earth. An asteroid is a chunk of rock from space. In the Gulf of Mexico, scientists have found a crater, or hole, that must have been made by an asteroid. If an asteroid hit the Earth, bits of earth would have flown into the air, causing great clouds of dust. The dust would have shaded the sun, causing plants to stop growing and bringing colder weather. Some animals and plants would have died from the cold or from the chemicals in the air. The animals that ate those plants and the animals that ate those animals would have died. A few other scientists think that these kinds of changes might have happened because of volcanoes or more gradual changes in weather.

Whatever the cause, many species of animals and plants disappeared at this time. Sue herself had died long before this great extinction. But other *Tyrannosaurus rex* were still living just before the extinction. Afterwards, no individual of the *T. rex* species ever lived again on Earth.

The animals that we usually call dinosaurs lived on Earth for about 165 million years all together. But to be perfectly correct, dinosaurs never did completely die out. Some survived and adapted and evolved and still live on Earth today. They are birds. All birds are living dinosaurs. Birds first evolved from their dinosaur ancestry during the Jurassic Period, and birds have continued to develop and thrive ever since. Bird skeletons look amazingly like those of *Tyrannosaurus rex*.

Like *Tyrannosaurus rex*, birds stand on two legs and have some hollow bones. Today's birds are the closest living relatives of *T. rex* — even closer than alligators and other reptiles. The next time you see a crow or a sparrow, think of their cousin Sue!

Comparison of a T. rex *skeleton and a bird's skeleton, showing some of the shared features that support an evolutionary origin of birds from dinosaurs.*
1) long, narrow scapula (shoulder blade) 2) hindlimbs (back legs) point straight downwards from the hip socket, not out to the side 3) S-shaped curve to the neck

CHAPTER 3
A Huge Job

The moving truck carrying Sue's bones pulled up at The Field Museum in October 1997. Everyone at the museum was excited. The crates were unloaded. Most crates were covered in plastic, and everyone could see the plaster-covered bones inside. From the size and number of the crates, everyone could also see what a big job was ahead!

One by one, the crates were pried open. The bones, in their plaster jackets, were lifted out. They had traveled well.

Now The Field Museum set up a new research laboratory where a lot of the real work would happen—the McDonald's Fossil Preparation Lab. Here, preparators would clean and prepare the bones. Glass windows let museum visitors watch them work. A camera connected to a computer let people all over the world watch the work on the museum's Web site. Another Field Museum laboratory was set up at Walt Disney World's Animal Kingdom. With ten full-time preparators at two state-of-the-art labs working on the bones, the museum hoped to finish the preparation in about two years. Both the labs and preparators of The Field

Museum were some of the finest in the world.

Every single bone needed to be cleaned and studied. It was a job that would take enormous skill and care. First, the preparators removed the plaster jacket from each bone. They used a cast saw, the very same kind of saw that doctors use to take a cast off a person's arm or leg. This special electric saw has a vibrating blade that cuts plaster but will not cut skin. The blade could cut the fossil bone, therefore, extreme care was used. The top half of the plaster jacket was carefully removed, along with the bone's foil wrapping. Sometimes preparators left the bottom half of the plaster on the bone. The plaster supported the bone as they cleaned the top half.

Underneath the plaster and foil, most of the bones were still surrounded by the matrix [MAY-tricks], the rock in which they were found. Preparators wanted to remove the matrix without making any mark at all on the fossilized bone underneath. Luckily, much of the matrix was sandstone, which was softer than the fossilized bones. Some of the matrix was siltstone or mudstone, which are also fairly soft. That made the job a little easier. But some of it was ironstone, which was tough to remove. So every move had to be made very carefully.

First, to remove the thickest layers of matrix, a preparator used a tiny jackhammer called an air scribe. This tool is normally used by engravers to carve words or pictures into metal. When its hard tip hits rock, it breaks the rock into tiny bits. If it touched the bone, this tip would damage the surface. So preparators used this tool only on thick layers of rock, not near the bone surface. They left a thin layer of rock still on the bone.

Now the work was even more delicate — the last layer of rock was right next to the bone. What tools should the preparators use to remove it? Before they started to remove the final layer, they tested tools to find out which would be the fastest and the safest. On a small patch of bone, preparators used a needle to remove the matrix. On another patch, they used a tiny sandblaster. A regular sandblaster shoots air and sand to remove material from a surface. But shooting sand at fossilized bones would damage them. So this smaller blaster shot a mixture of air and baking soda instead of sand. The Field Museum's scientists looked at the two cleaned patches of bone using a very powerful scanning electron microscope to magnify the bone thousands of times. They decided that the tiny blaster worked better than the needle. The baking soda used in the blaster was hard enough to remove the last of the sandstone, siltstone, or mudstone matrix. But it was soft enough so that it did not damage the bone.

In a few places, the matrix closest to the bone was ironstone. Ironstone actually does contain iron and is much harder than sandstone. It was only slightly softer than the fossilized bones. So the ironstone matrix was the most difficult to remove. Baking soda did not remove it. Instead, preparators put tiny glass beads in the blaster. The glass beads removed the ironstone, but they could also damage the bones, so preparators had to be especially careful.

right: The Field Museum preparators at work.

The preparators used other tools that normally would be used by dentists or jewelers: drills, picks, pins, and blowers. They used magnifying glasses and even microscopes to look closely at the bones. They wanted to be sure that they removed only rock, not bone. How did they know the difference? The fossilized bones were darker, heavier, smoother, and harder than the matrix.

As the preparators removed the matrix, bits of rock and dirt flew into the air. The scientists tested the matrix to be sure that there was nothing in it that would be harmful to the preparators. They found a small amount of an especially hazardous form of silica, a white material that is found in sand. Silica dust could be harmful to breathe. So, when the preparators were using power tools to remove the matrix, they wore masks so that they would not breathe the dust. They also wore goggles to protect their eyes. Big pipes pulled the dusty air out of the room, like huge vacuum cleaners.

The two teams of preparators had an enormous job. They had to clean, very carefully, every tiny spot on more than 250 *Tyrannosaurus rex* bones. If they made even a small mistake, a piece of 67-million-year-old bone would be lost forever. So work was slow and careful. Just one bone might take a preparator several weeks of hard work. The skull took a team of four people almost six months to finish!

below & right: The Field Museum team carefully prepares Sue's skull and jaws.

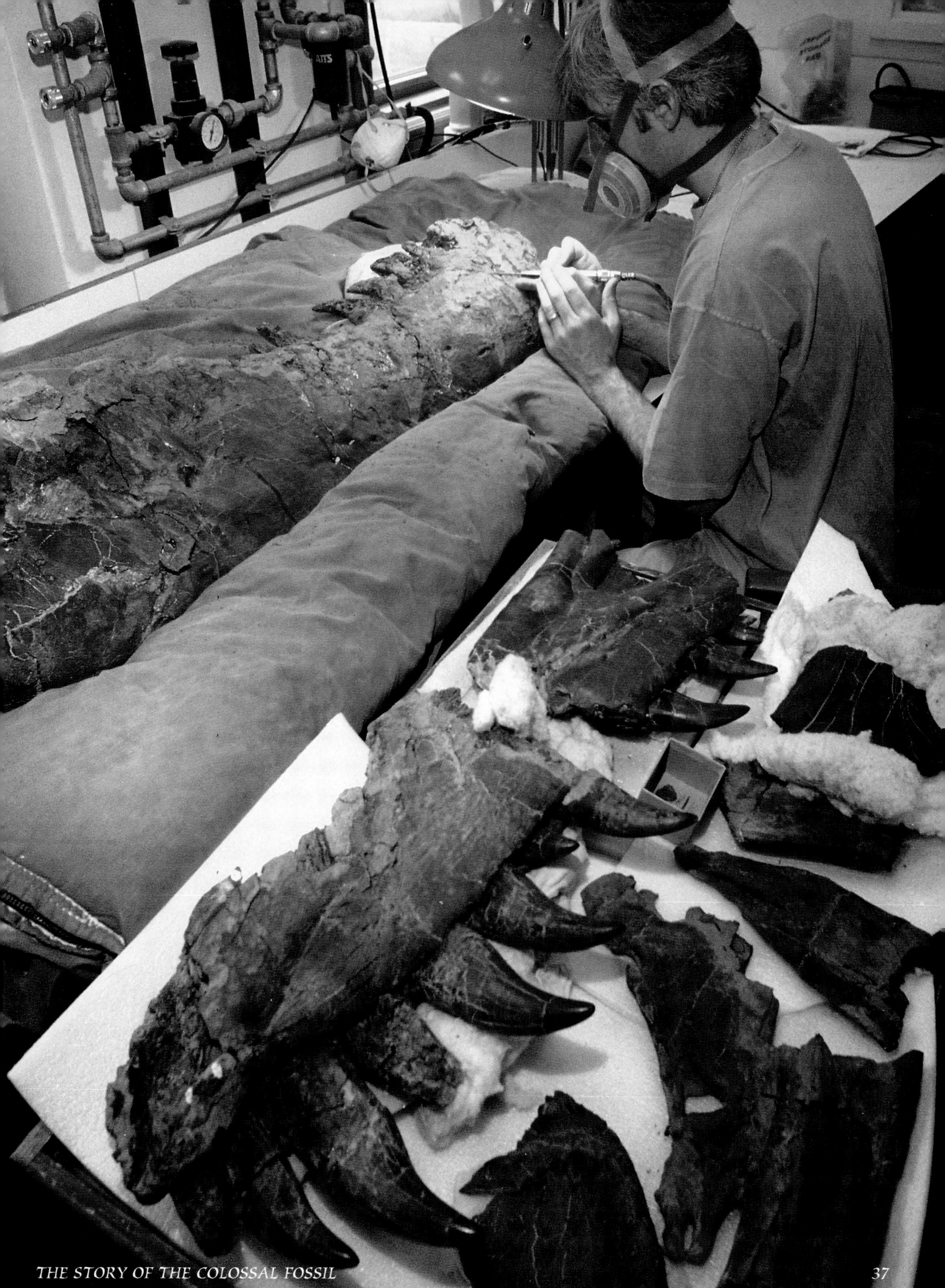

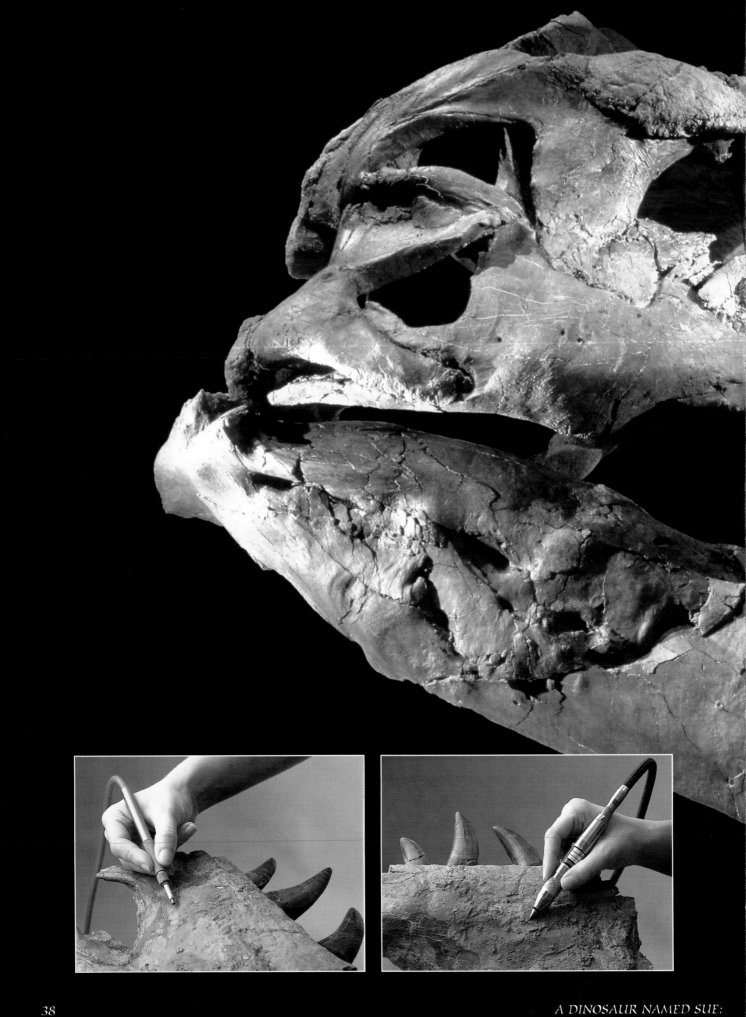

A DINOSAUR NAMED SUE:

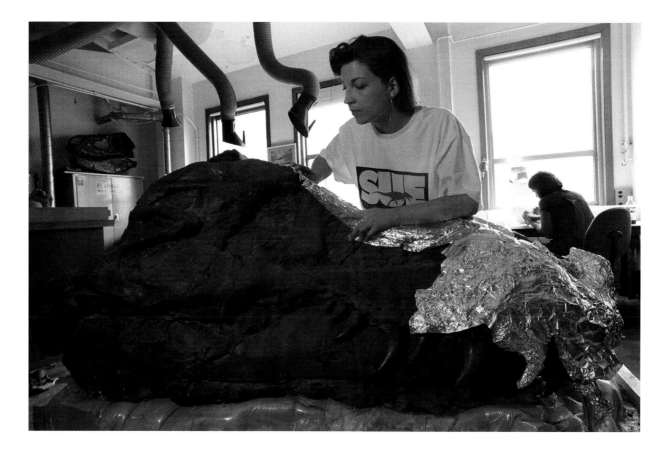

As the preparators worked on cleaning the bones, the museum's research paleontologists started their studies. They measured and photographed each bone. They looked closely at spots where muscles had been attached. They looked at places where Sue's bones had been injured. They wanted very much to look inside the bones, too.

Years ago, when scientists wanted to look inside a fossilized bone, they had to break it open. No one wanted to break Sue's bones. The Field Museum scientists had a better idea. They would put some of the bones in a computed tomography [toe-MAH-gruh-fee], or CT, scanner. This is a modern machine that is usually used to let doctors look inside the bodies of live patients without hurting them. It takes X-ray pictures in a series of "slices." Then a computer puts all of the pictures together to create a three-dimensional picture of the inside of a human body—or a dinosaur bone.

The Field Museum scientists were most eager to look inside Sue's skull. But the skull was so big that it would not fit inside a medical CT scanner at a hospital. Where could they find a really big CT scanner? Boeing Corporation had a giant and more powerful CT scanner that it used to look for hidden problems inside airplane engines or space shuttle parts. Sue's skull could fit inside that CT scanner—but just barely!

Sue's skull was prepared for the trip to Boeing's Rocketdyne laboratory in Ventura County, California. The skull would have to tip on end inside the scanner. So most of the rocky matrix was left inside the skull to support it. Normally, a fossil might be packed in sand to support it as it turned inside the CT scanner. But Sue's skull, plus extra sand, would be too heavy for Boeing's scanner. The preparators had to use a lighter packing material. So first they covered the skull in foil. Then they sprayed a thick coating of plastic foam over the whole skull. The workers wore special suits and breathing gear, because the foam would give off poisonous gas.

Next, an engineer designed a special crate to be built by The Field Museum staff. Sue's skull would stay inside the crate during scanning. So the crate had to be strong enough to protect the skull as it rotated inside the scanner. It also had to be small enough to fit inside the scanner. Finally, the crate was loaded on another moving van and sent to California.

The entire crate was loaded into the CT machine and was rotated so that it stood on end, nose up. Then the scientists began to take X-ray pictures. The X-rays went right through the crate, the foam, and the foil to take a picture of the bones. Each picture showed a "slice" of Sue's skull, as if the skull were a huge loaf of bread. It took more than a month to take pictures of the entire five-foot-long skull. The scientists took nearly 750 X-ray pictures. A computer put all of the pictures together to form a 3-D model of what Sue's skull and jaws looked like, both outside and inside. Then the skull was carefully shipped back to The Field Museum in Chicago.

right & below: Sue's skull is readied for its journey by truck to California.

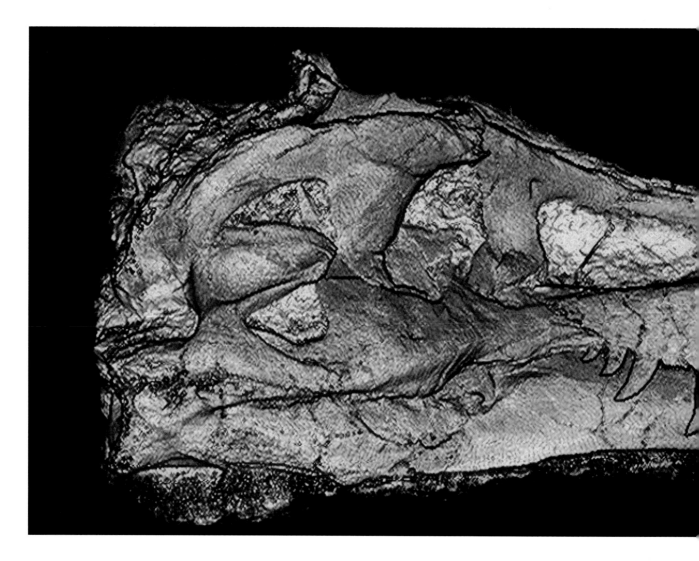

The computer pictures gave museum scientists lots of information. Preparators had left the rock, or matrix, inside the skull. Now, as they started to clean out the matrix inside the skull, they looked at the CT scan to see exactly where the rock ended and the bone or teeth began. Chris Brochu, The Field Museum's lead Sue researcher, "sliced up" skull images to show the inside of Sue's skull. He looked closely at the CT pictures to measure the size of Sue's brain and other parts of her head. Never before had scientists had so much information about the head of *Tyrannosaurus rex*.

The CT scan of Sue's skull was so interesting that the museum's scientists wanted to scan some other bones, too. Some of Sue's bones had unusual lumps or bumps or holes. By looking inside the bones, they hoped to see whether the strange spots were caused by a break that had healed, an infection, or something else. They also wanted to learn more about the shapes and positions of the bones. So a rib, a piece of another rib, and bones from Sue's arm and leg were taken to a hospital not far from The Field Museum. These smaller bones were packed in bubble wrap and carefully driven to the hospital.

At the hospital, doctors put Sue's bones into a CT X-ray scanner to get a 3-D picture of the inside of the bones. These were the same kind of X-ray pictures that doctors might take of a patient's broken bone. Now The Field Museum paleontologists would be able to study these bones both inside and out.

---

above right & left: Chris Brochu, Field Museum paleontologist, studies the results of the CT scans of Sue's skull.

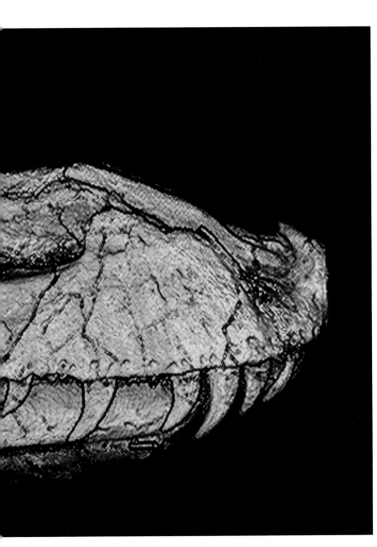

*middle right: Boeing
technicians view scans
of the skull.
right: The skull (inside
the crate) is rotated
and placed on the
scanner bed.*

As studies continued, preparators started to get the bones ready to display in the museum. They fixed small cracks in the bones with a special type of glue. This glue, or epoxy, flows as easily as water and was used to strengthen the cracks.

Broken pieces of bone needed to be put together, like a big jigsaw puzzle. Preparators placed the bones in position in a box of sand. The sand supported the bones while the preparators glued the pieces together.

Bits were missing from some bones. Preparators pushed a brownish-red compound, a little like modeling clay, into the cracks to fill in these gaps. The compound started out soft, but it dried hard and tough, like bone. Its reddish color was different from the dark brown of the bones themselves. That way, everyone could tell what parts were real bone, and what parts had been added.

A few of Sue's bones were missing altogether. One arm, one foot, and a few vertebrae [VER-tuh-bray], or backbones, were never found. In order to show what Sue's complete skeleton looked like, the preparators modeled new bones out of plastic. They could use the bones they had as models. To make a left arm for Sue, for example, they took laser pictures of the bones of Sue's right arm. A computer turned those pictures around to show what Sue's left arm would have looked like. Following those measurements, a specialized machine made a new left arm for Sue. They then sculpted all the details that would be found on a real bone, but they made the new bones a reddish color, so that everyone would know that they were not Sue's own bones.

Preparators also made several exact copies, or casts, of each bone. First, they painted a goo called silicone rubber onto the bone. Silicone rubber would come off the bone easily, without damaging it. They made sure that the rubber coated every surface of the bone. A hard, plastic-like material was put around the rubber mold to support it. They carefully removed the two halves of the rubber block from the bone. The empty space inside the rubber block was exactly the size and shape of the real bone. This was the mold.

The museum sent the molds to a company, Research Casting International, that would make the casts. There, workers filled the mold with a mixture of liquid plastic and fiberglass. This mixture became hard as it dried. Again, they painted the first layer in so that the mixture would reach into every tiny corner of the mold. Then they poured more of the mixture in and put the two halves of the mold together.

When the mixture was dry, they carefully removed the mold. They trimmed off any extra plastic. Now they had a cast, an exact copy of the original bone. The copies are so good that scientists can see every tiny crack and bump that they could see on the real bones. The museum kept at least one cast of each bone. Scientists can use these copies for most kinds of study. This way, they seldom need to remove a real bone from the museum's display. That means less wear and tear on the real bones, and more chances for museum visitors to see all of Sue's real bones on display.

One set of casts would go to Florida. There, at Disney's Animal Kingdom, a copy of Sue's entire skeleton would be put on display. The Field Museum would send two more complete copies of Sue's skeleton on tour to many places in the country in a traveling show sponsored by the McDonald's Corporation. McDonald's generosity will allow millions of people to have the chance to see and learn about this magnificent fossil specimen.

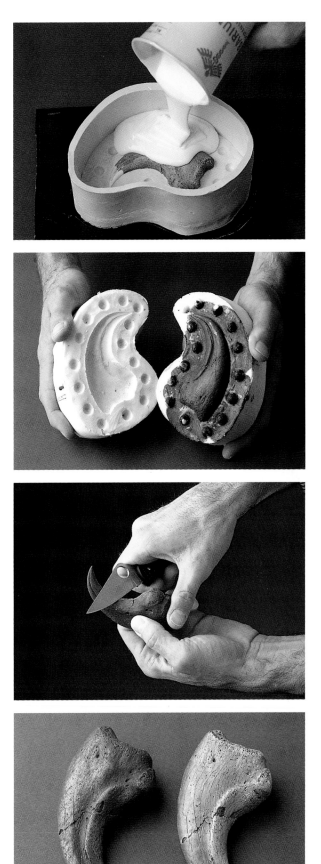

right: Steps in the normal molding and casting process; the same process was used for Sue's bones.
left: A California State University student intern prepares a bone for molding.

CHAPTER 4

Putting the Puzzle Together

Now that the bones were cleaned and repaired, there was another huge job to do: putting all the pieces together. They needed to fit all the bones in their proper places and figure out how to display the whole skeleton at The Field Museum in Chicago.

There was no space at The Field Museum to put together a skeleton that was bigger than a school bus! Also, there are very few experts in the world who know how to put a big skeleton together for a museum display. One of the best experts, Phil Fraley, was in the New York City area. So The Field Museum packed up Sue's bones again and sent them to a big building in New Jersey. There, Phil and his team could do the mounting work on Sue. The building is usually used by artists to create big sculptures. The metal stand supporting Sue was about to become the biggest sculpture of all. And what a sculpture! This one would display the real bones of

the world's largest two-legged dinosaur skeleton!

The Field Museum's scientists had already figured out what each bone was. Each bone had a number. You might think that it would be easy to put the bones together. But this puzzle was more difficult than any jigsaw puzzle!

Each piece of this puzzle was a heavy, fossilized bone. Just getting the skeleton to stand up was a big challenge. Most dinosaur skeleton displays are casts or models of bones. These copies are easier to put together because they are light and because people can drill holes into them. They can bolt them together or put them on poles. But nearly all of Sue's bones were real bones. The Field Museum would not allow holes to be drilled in Sue's precious bones.

Phil would have to design a special frame to hold the bones up without damaging them. There was one more big challenge: The Field Museum's scientists wanted to be able to remove any bone at any time without taking down the whole skeleton.

Of course, the bones also needed to fit together correctly, as they had when Sue was alive. Until the bones actually went together, scientists would not be sure how long or how tall Sue really was.

Scientists had to decide how Sue would stand. The pose needed to be realistic — showing something that a *Tyrannosaurus rex* really would do. It should be exciting for museum visitors to see, giving them a real feeling for what the living animal was like. And the skeleton needed to be in a position that was practical to build. They decided to show Sue as if she were moving forward and crouched a little, perhaps about to feed on or attack another animal. The pose shows Sue as she is interrupted, surprised by something off to her side.

---

below: The fully prepared skull and jaws are being readied for transport and mounting.
opposite: Field Museum scientists piece together Sue's ribs.

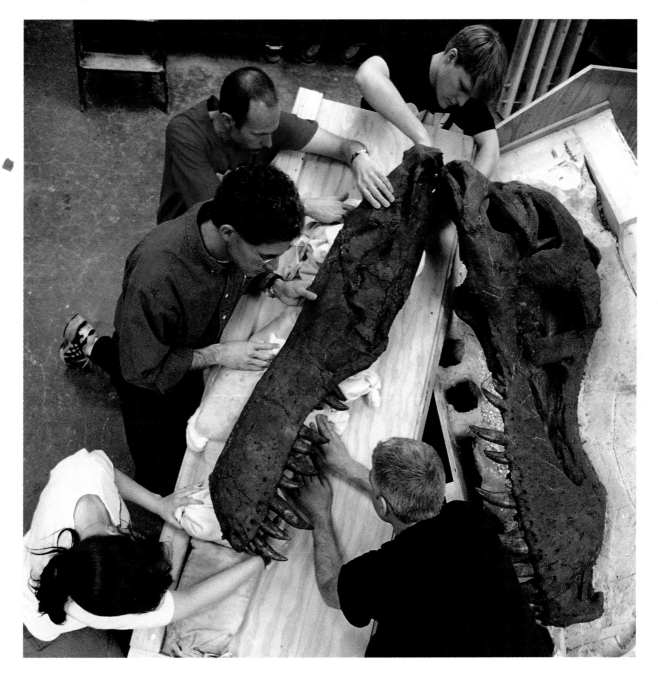

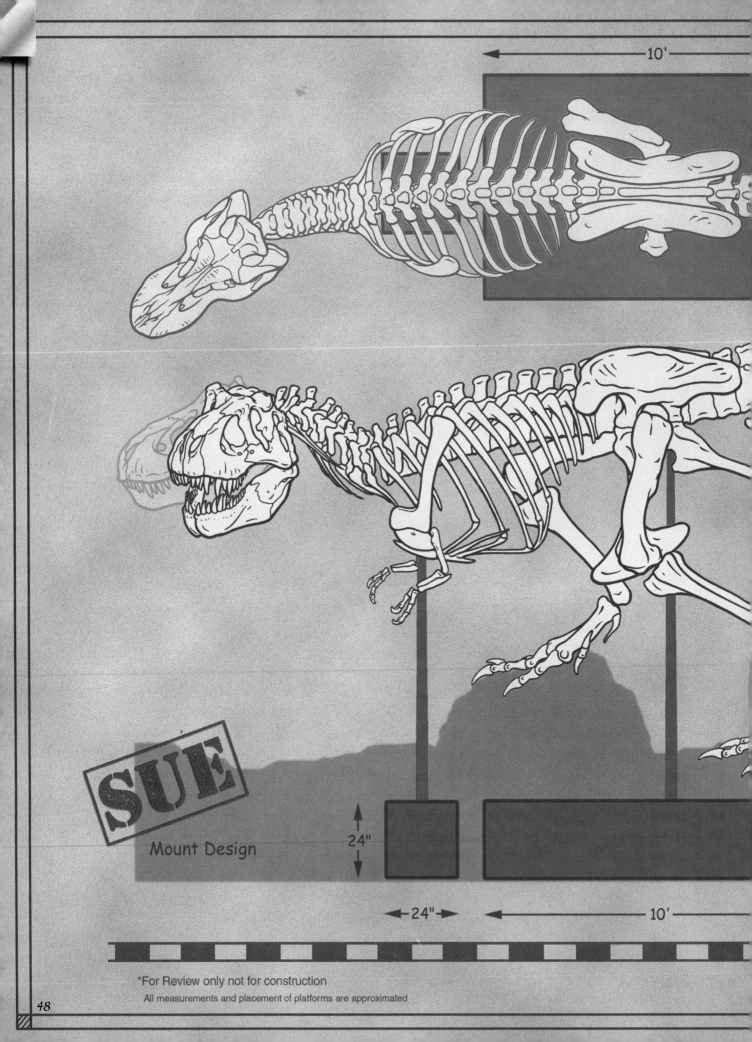

10'

24"

SUE

Mount Design

24"

10'

*For Review only not for construction

All measurements and placement of platforms are approximated

48

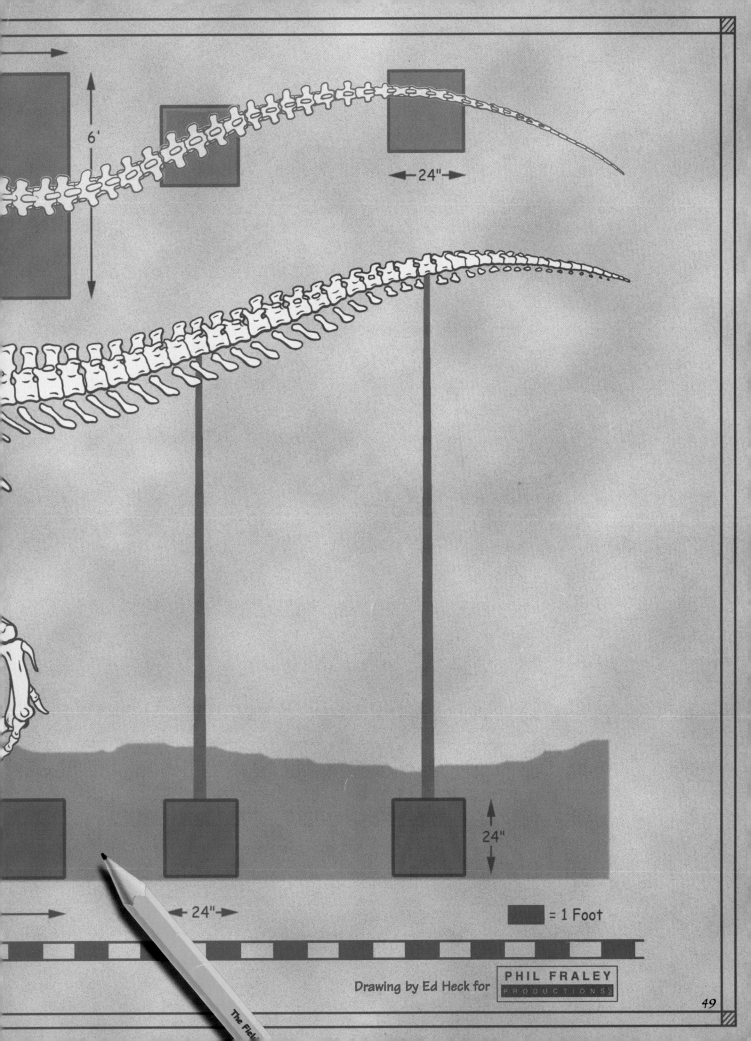

6'

24"

24"

24"

24"

= 1 Foot

Drawing by Ed Heck for PHIL FRALEY PRODUCTIONS

In New Jersey, the museum's staff worked with Phil Fraley's team to draft many drawings and then build a small model of Sue's skeleton. The model showed each bone and the metal pieces needed to hold each bone in place. This would be a map for building Sue's real skeleton.

Work began to build the steel frame, or armature [AR-muh-chur], that would hold the bones in position. A scaffold gave workers a place to stand as they put together the higher parts of the skeleton. A hoist lifted the heavy bones into place.

Since the skeleton would be on open display in a museum, the bones had to be held firmly and safely in place. Yet the bones needed to be easy to remove. So, for each bone, metal workers made a small but sturdy and beautiful steel holder. Like a skinny hand, each holder had fingers to keep the bone in place. But, if necessary, the bone could be removed without damage.

The holders were painted a brownish color—a color slightly different from the bones. That way, museum visitors would be able to tell what was bone and what was metal.

Then the metal holders were linked together with steel rods. Piece by piece, the armature went together like a huge, strange sculpture. How would the whole thing stand up? The center of the skeleton was the pelvis, or hip bones. The holder for these bones would be attached to a large post and secured to the floor of the museum. This would be the one part of the skeleton most difficult to remove for study. Other supports were added wherever needed to hold up the weight of the bones and armature.

The SUE Science Team from The Field Museum traveled to New Jersey to evaluate the progress of mounting Sue's bones. They worked with Phil Fraley and his team to finalize details of the pose.

A DINOSAUR NAMED SUE:

One big problem for the skeleton builders was Sue's skull. It was so heavy that it was impossible to fasten it up high, where Sue's neck would be. Also, if the skull were up high, visitors would not be able to look at it closely. The scientists thought of a way to solve these problems.

A very special cast was made of Sue's skull. This copy would not be an exact copy of the real skull. Sue's real skull had been buried under many layers of earth and stone for millions of years. It was distorted in places, although less broken than most fossilized skulls that have been found. But, in addition, parts of the fossilized bones of the skull had actually stretched out of shape. The skull had been squashed and was slightly flattened. It did not look exactly the way it did when Sue was alive. So the museum scientists decided to make a special cast to show what the skull had looked like 67 million years ago, before it was squashed.

The preparators made this plastic cast of Sue's skull by cutting apart the original cast of the distorted skull and gluing it back together to correct the distortion. Then they heated and stretched some areas and carved away some parts inside so that they could put the skull back into its original shape. They would put that cast high up on Sue's skeleton for display in the museum. That way, people could see what Sue's whole skeleton really looked like when she was alive. It also solved the other problems. The plastic cast was much lighter and easier to hang up for display. And they could put Sue's real skull in a special case on the second floor of the museum. There, visitors could get very close and see all the details of the spectacular teeth, jaws, and skull bones.

At last the bones were ready. The armature was built. The whole skeleton was put together in the New Jersey workshop. Everyone cheered! The finished skeleton was forty-one feet (thirteen meters) long from nose to tail. Sue stood twelve feet (four meters) tall at the hips. Even the people who had worked on Sue for more than two years were amazed at the sight of this astounding skeleton.

One last time, the bones were taken down and packed in crates. One last time, they were shipped by truck to The Field Museum. The armature was taken apart in large pieces, and it rode with the bones to Chicago.

The mounting team moved in, set up shop, and began to put the bones and armature together again. Slowly, Sue began to take shape. The Field Museum will build a new, custom-designed exhibit hall especially for Sue. But, until then, Sue will be the star of the museum's famous Stanley Field Hall.

In May 2000, almost ten years after Susan Hendrickson spotted those few bones, dinosaur Sue's skeleton stood up tall and fearsome in her new home. Now, it does not take much imagination to see how awesome Sue had been in life!

---

below: Field Museum scientists at work preparing the cast of Sue's skull.
opposite: Field Museum scientists position part of Sue's upper eye socket that was crushed during fossilization.

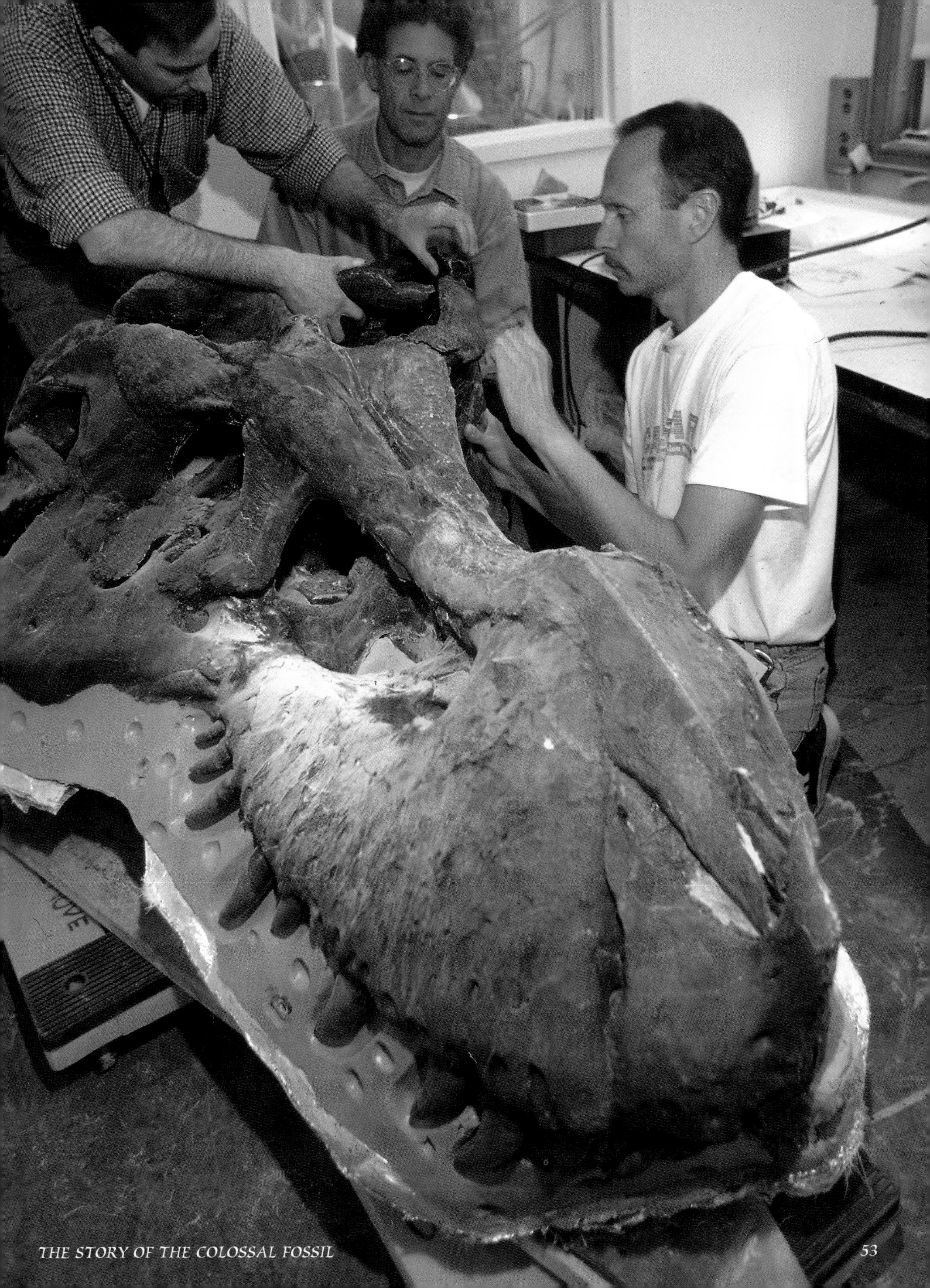

© 2000 The Field Museum

CHAPTER 5
Learning From Sue

Sue's skeleton is an amazing sight. But it is much, much more than that. Scientists around the world are thrilled to have the chance to study Sue's bones. Why was Sue such an important discovery?

Field Museum paleontologists have already learned a lot more about *Tyrannosaurus rex* because of the completeness of Sue's skeleton and the beautiful preservation of the bones. Many of these bones had never been found in a *T. rex* before, such as the almost complete set of rib-like bones surrounding the belly, a six-inch-long ear bone that transmitted sound, and a pair of tiny bones attached to the back of the skull. There is even a whole series of air sacs in the skull and vertebrae that had never been seen in this species. New techniques, like CT scanning, tell us that Sue had gigantic olfactory [all-FAK-

turee] bulbs on the brain, and that smell, not sight, was the dominant way that Sue sensed her environment.

One of the most important things we have been able to learn from Sue is that there are many new features showing that birds are living relatives of the meat-eating dinosaurs. CT scans show that two tiny passageways in the side of the skull are arranged just like in birds (not crocodiles, as was previously believed). The hips are so well preserved that Field Museum paleontologists were able to reconstruct exact arrangements of leg muscles. Scientists had suspected that certain muscles were present in *T. rex*, but there was no definite evidence of them before. Now, on Sue, they could see exactly where the muscles had attached on her bones. And again, the particular

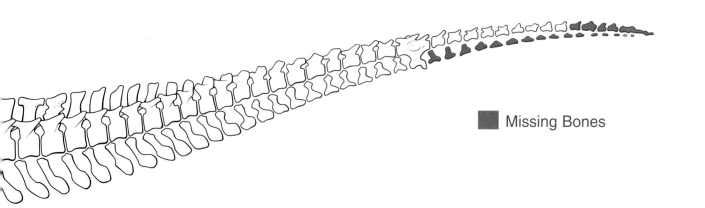

muscles and their positions on the legs and hips are just like in birds!

At The Field Museum, as chief preparator Bill Simpson studied Sue's bones, he discovered a rib bone that had never been seen before in a *Tyrannosaurus rex* find. This discovery immediately added to what scientists know about the anatomy of *T. rex*.

Sue's skeleton was also the largest *Tyrannosaurus rex* skeleton ever found. It may give scientists new clues about how *T. rex* managed to find enough food to support its huge body. Was *T. rex* a hunter or a scavenger? Sue may finally give an answer to that question.

Because Sue was the largest *Tyrannosaurus rex* ever found, we know that she was probably the oldest when she died. This may be the first chance to study the effects of old age on a *T. rex*!

Most of Sue's bones were in excellent condition. By looking closely at scars and marks on the outside of the bones and details on the inside of the bones, Field Museum scientists can learn more about the kinds of diseases and injuries that might have affected the skeleton of *Tyrannosaurus rex*. Perhaps they can even figure out why Sue died.

Sue's bones were not the only fossils found in the area. Fossils of plants and other animals—including other dinosaurs—found near Sue may tell scientists many things about the time when Sue lived. What was the climate like? What plants and animals lived nearby? What did Sue eat?

The Field Museum scientists were lucky. They were able to use X-rays and CT scans to look inside Sue's bones—something that was impossible for paleontologists 100 years ago.

The scans of Sue's skull have already told these paleontologists a lot about *Tyrannosaurus rex*. They used a computer to put the CT scan pictures together to show a 3-D model of the inside of the skull. So far, the museum's scientists have learned that Sue's brain sat in a space that was about the size of a quart of milk—one foot (thirty centimeters) long. That does not tell us how smart Sue was. But scientists can learn which parts of the brain were most important—the parts for thinking, seeing, smelling, or moving, for instance.

Chris Brochu is The Field Museum paleontologist who wrote the scientific report on the complete skeleton of Sue. This is the first complete scientific report on *Tyrannosaurus rex* ever published, even though the species has been known for nearly 100 years! When Chris looked at the CT scan of Sue's skull, he was amazed. He saw that the parts of the brain involved in smell (the olfactory bulbs) were *huge*—bigger than the entire remainder of the brain! Sue must have been able to smell things from very far away, and in great detail! Probably no animal, living or dead, could have stayed hidden from Sue's nose. That does not help us figure out whether Sue hunted live animals or ate dead ones. A great sense of smell would be helpful either way. But it does tell us that Sue must have been able to "see" the world in a way that humans cannot. Hundreds of smells constantly told Sue about everything all around her.

Sue's bones showed quite a few scars — places where the bones might have been injured in some way and then healed. When diggers first found the skeleton, they wondered whether Sue had been in a big fight. Perhaps that was how she had died! But Chris Brochu looked very carefully at all of the injuries. He looked at the X-rays and CT scans of Sue's bones. He found nothing to show that Sue had been in a fight. Most of the scars were probably caused by infections — invasions by germs — or cancers. Some scars were found on Sue's jaws. A hole in the upper bone of Sue's right arm was probably caused by an infection. Her leg and tail might also have had infections. CT scans lead scientists to believe that Sue may have had some disease, injury, or trauma to her tail. Scientists do not know exactly what caused these infections. The germs we know today might have been different in the Cretaceous Period! That will be an important subject for scientists to continue to study.

Some of Sue's ribs seemed to have broken and healed. No one knows for sure what caused those breaks. People can break their ribs by falling, by being hit, or sometimes even by coughing too hard. With more studies, scientists may be able to make a better guess about what happened to Sue's ribs.

One paleontologist was especially interested in Sue's arms. Sue's arms were short — too short to reach her mouth, for example. How did Sue use her arms? Or were they useless? He looked closely at the spots on the bones where Sue's muscles had been attached. Those spots have ridges. From the size and shape of those spots, he could tell that her arm muscles must have been quite large and very strong. If Sue's arms had been useless, the muscles would not have been strong. Scientists hope that more studies on Sue's bones will solve the mystery of how *Tyrannosaurus rex* used their arms.

---

above: Scientist Chris Brochu studies Sue's skull.
*opposite: The fibula bone on the right shows evidence
of abnormal growth when compared
with the normal fibula of Sue.*

As scientists study Sue's bones, they also study the other fossils found nearby. These fossils show which plants and animals were alive at exactly the same time as Sue. They can give an excellent picture of how Sue lived about 67 million years ago.

Some fossilized leaves and pieces of wood were actually found inside Sue's mouth. That does not mean that Sue was eating them when she died. The pieces landed there after Sue died, as the skeleton was quickly covered with sand and mud. But these pieces definitely came from plants that were alive at the same time as Sue. Pinecones, pine branches, and other leaves were found mixed with Sue's bones.

Fossils of other animals were also nearby. A fossilized turtle head was found among Sue's bones in the original discovery. Near Sue's skeleton were more *Tyrannosaurus rex* bones, some from a young dinosaur. Were these animals related to Sue? Did *T. rex* live in groups or alone? As study continues, scientists may find out.

---

opposite: The rocky matrix that held Sue contained fossilized records of many plants and animals that lived at the same time as she did. below: Turtle skull, found while excavating Sue.

middle right: The humerus bone of a lizard-like animal found with Sue.
middle left and bottom right: Leaves found in the matrix surrounding Sue.
bottom left: Lacrimal (skull bone) from the face of a baby tyrannosaur found with Sue.

THE STORY OF THE COLOSSAL FOSSIL

The scientists of The Field Museum will continue to study Sue's skeleton for many years to come. Perhaps they will be able to solve some of the remaining mysteries. For instance, what can Sue tell us about the evolutionary connection between dinosaurs and birds? Exactly how old was Sue when she died?

A question that many people wonder about is what *Tyrannosaurus rex* skin looked like. Because skin usually rots and usually does not change to fossil, no one really knows. In artwork, people often show *T. rex* with skin that looks green or brown or gray, like many of today's reptiles. But that is just a guess. *T. rex* skin might have been red or purple! It might have had wild patterns or patches of feathers! Different kinds of dinosaurs might have been different colors. For now, we have to use our imagination to picture the skin and color of Sue. One sculptor, Brian Cooley, worked with the museum's scientists to make a model of Sue's skull for The Field Museum. He added muscle, eyes, and skin to show what Sue's head might have looked like. Scientists believe that his model is a very good guess. Museum scientists worked with another artist, John Gurche, to develop the lifelike painting of Sue on pages 10 and 11 of this book.

Other mysteries remain. Did *Tyrannosaurus rex* hunt live animals? Did they eat already-dead animals? Or both? Did *T. rex* live its life mainly alone? Or did these dinosaurs live in groups? Were dinosaurs warm-blooded or cold-blooded? The work of Field Museum scientists on Sue's bones may help to find answers to these questions.

Now Sue's skeleton is on display at The Field Museum in Chicago. There, anyone can stand next to her 67-million-year-old bones and imagine what she was like when she was alive. Scientists from around the world can look at the skeleton and study the bones. Thousands more people can see the exact copies of the skeleton in Florida or in the touring exhibits.

At The Field Museum, scientists will continue their work. They will make a more detailed computer map of Sue's skull for scientists around the world to use. They will take more CT scans of Sue's bones. They will write more reports and books about Sue. As they learn about Sue, everyone's ideas about *T. rex* will continue to change.

Museum educators will plan programs to help children and adults learn more about Sue and the world in which *Tyrannosaurus rex* lived. Some of the children who see Sue today may even become the paleontologists of tomorrow.

And, if all those things happen, then Sue is still alive!

above: John Flynn, Chairman of the Geology Department at The Field Museum, lecturing on Sue. opposite: Sculpture by Brian Cooley showing what Sue might have looked like.

A DINOSAUR NAMED SUE:

After 67 million years and thousands of hours
of preparation, restoration, and study,
Sue stands again, her mounting complete.

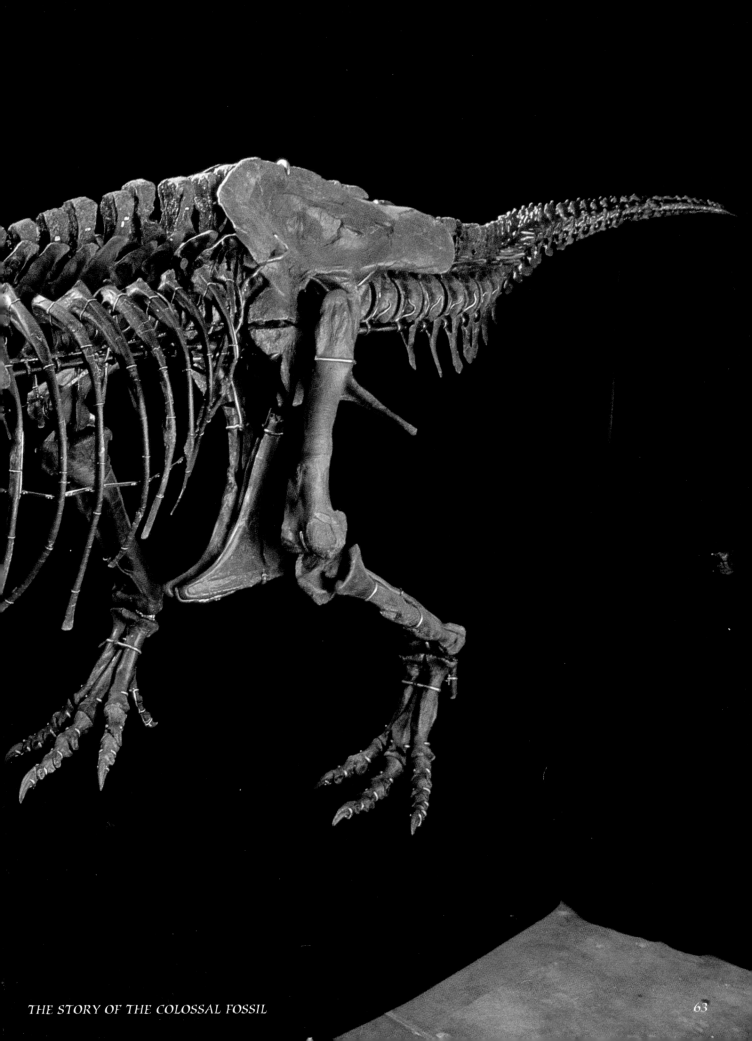

INDEX